W9-AZF-660

Jane Eyre

Artists: Penko Gelev
Sotir Gelev

First edition for North America (including Canada and Mexico), Philippine Islands, and Puerto Rico published in 2009 by Barron's Educational Series, Inc.

© The Salariya Book Company Limited 2009
All rights reserved. No part of this publication may be reproduced or distributed in any form or by any means without the written permission of the copyright owner.

This book is being sold subject to the condition that it shall not be resold or otherwise circulated in any binding or cover other than that in which it was originally published without the copyright holder's consent.

All inquiries should be addressed to:
Barron's Educational Series, Inc.
250 Wireless Blvd.
Hauppauge, NY 11788
www.barronseduc.com

ISBN-13 (Hardcover): 978-0-7641-6142-1
ISBN-10 (Hardcover): 0-7641-6142-3
ISBN-13 (Paperback): 978-0-7641-4011-2
ISBN-10 (Paperback): 0-7641-4011-6

Library of Congress Control No.: 2008936597

Picture credits:
p. 46 The British Library/HIP/TopFoto
p. 47 © Topham Picturepoint/TopFoto.co.uk
Every effort has been made to trace copyright holders. The Salariya Book Company apologizes for any omissions and would be pleased, in such cases, to add an acknowledgement in future editions.

Printed and bound in China
9 8 7 6 5 4 3 2 1

Jane Eyre

Charlotte Brontë

Illustrated by

Penko Gelev

Retold by

Fiona Macdonald

Series created and designed by

David Salariya

"My strength is quite failing me. I cannot go much further. Shall I be an outcast again this night? While the rain descends so, must I lay my head on the cold, drenched ground?"

(See page 37)

CHARACTERS

Jane Eyre

Mrs Sarah Reed, Jane's aunt

Eliza, Jane's cousin

Georgiana, Jane's cousin

John, Jane's cousin

Mr Lloyd, a local doctor

Mr Brocklehurst,
the schoolmaster

Helen Burns,
Jane's schoolfriend

Edward Fairfax Rochester,
master of Thornfield Hall

Mrs Fairfax, the
housekeeper

Adèle Varens,
Jane's pupil

Grace Poole,
serving woman

St John, the priest

Diana, the priest's sister

Mary, the priest's sister

AN UNHAPPY ORPHAN

November 1837

Each picture tells a story.

Gateshead House, north England

Why am I always suffering?

Jane Eyre, an orphan of about 9 years old, sits alone reading. Her cousins, Eliza and Georgiana Reed, are playing in the next room. Their mother, Mrs. Sarah Reed, fondly looks on. She spoils those children—and Jane is banned from joining them!

Jane feels hurt, sad, and angry. She is happier alone.

Wicked and cruel boy! You are like a murderer!

Boh! You rat!

Rat! Rat! Owwww!!

What a fury! Take her to the Red Room!

Jane's cousin John Reed stomps into the room and attacks Jane. He's a spoiled, stupid bully.

Mrs. Reed hurries into the room. She blames Jane for the fight.

For shame! What shocking conduct!

She's like a mad cat!

Unjust! Unjust!

Jane kicks and struggles as two maids, Bessie and Abbot, march her away to the sinister Red Room. Her uncle, Mr. Reed, died there!

My uncle's spirit! A ghost!

Night falls. Is that moonlight flickering in the mirror?

Jane begs to be let out, but Mrs. Reed refuses. Left alone all night in the haunted room, Jane faints in terror.

TROUBLES AT HOME

The next day...

Jane wakes up in the nursery, confused and frightened. Mr. Lloyd, the local apothecary,[1] is sitting by her bedside. Bessie stands close by.

Would you like to drink, or could you eat anything?

Wonderful civility![2]

Utter wretchedness...

Jane soon feels stronger, and is well enough to get up and sit by the fire. But her mind is still in turmoil. She can't stop crying.

Have you any pain?

I cry because I am miserable.

Mr. Lloyd gently talks to Jane. He's worried; Jane ought to look more cheerful!

The child ought to have a change of air and scene.

I'll gladly get rid of such a tiresome, ill-conditioned[3] child.

Mr. Lloyd reports to Mrs. Reed. He thinks Jane should leave Gateshead House—and go to boarding school!

Grandfather Reed cut her off without a shilling...

Bessie and Abbot gossip about Jane's parents.

Jane's father was a priest, and her mother came from a rich family. But they disapproved of the marriage, and disowned her.

Poor Miss Jane is to be pitied...

Both Jane's parents died of a deadly disease that they caught while helping poor people.

School... school!

Slowly, Jane grows stronger. But she still desperately wants to leave Gateshead House.

They are not fit to associate with *me!*

She is not worthy of notice.

John Reed tries to bully Jane again. Mrs. Reed tells all her children to avoid and ignore Jane—and Jane loses her temper!

1. apothecary: pharmacist and junior doctor.
2. civility: politeness.
3. ill-conditioned: bad-tempered.

Papa and Mamma are in heaven...

...they can see all you do and think... and how you wish me dead!

Mrs. Reed is furious. She chases Jane upstairs, shakes her, and hits her.

It's Christmas time, but Jane is banned from all the celebrations. Shut away, all alone, she feels wicked—and rebellious.

Well, Jane Eyre, and are you a good child?

After Christmas, Mrs. Reed summons Mr. Brocklehurst, a schoolmaster.

Do you know where the wicked go after death?

Do you say your prayers? Do you read your Bible?

What a nose! What a mouth! And what large teeth!

Mr. Brocklehurst beckons Jane to come close, and fires questions at her. Jane is frightened, but defiant.

Keep a strict eye on her. Guard against her worst fault...deceit!

Mrs. Reed says that she is thinking of sending Jane to Mr. Brocklehurst's school. But first, she must warn him: Jane is wicked and violent! She must be kept humble, and taught to work hard.

I am not deceitful: I dislike you the worst of anybody in the world!

How dare you!

Jane is furious that she has been called a liar. Mrs. Reed is so unfair! Jane shouts at her.

You think I have no feelings, and that I can do without one bit of love or kindness...

...You are bad, hard hearted... Send me to school!

Jane is so angry that she is no longer afraid of her aunt. She continues to shout, passionately.

WELCOME TO LOWOOD

At last, Jane is to go to school. Bessie helps her to get ready. She is very kind; Jane is sorry to be leaving her.

Jane is to travel alone by coach. It's a long journey—fifty miles! When Jane reaches her new school, Lowood, she is exhausted and night has fallen.

At Lowood, a servant comes to meet Jane.

Inside, Jane is met by two teachers—young and kindly Miss Temple, and Miss Miller, who is older and care-worn.

Miss Miller leads Jane through a classroom full of girls.

She gives Jane some supper of cold water and oatcake[1]—then shows Jane to her bed in a large dormitory.[2]

Jane goes to sleep, exhausted.

---

1. oatcake: ground-up oat grains mixed with water, then baked into a hard, dry, biscuit.
2. dormitory: a large bedroom for many people in a school.

Early next morning, Jane and the other girls are wakened by a clanging bell.

It's still dark, but they have to get up and wash in icy water. After getting dressed, it's time for prayers. Jane feels weak from stress and hunger.

At last, breakfast is served—burned porridge! It's slimy, disgusting, and totally inedible.[2] Jane and the other girls are hungry and miserable.

The teachers arrive, ready to begin lessons.

Miss Temple, the headmistress, seems kind and calm. The other four teachers are far less friendly.

The girls look pale. Miss Temple asks why. When she hears about the porridge, she orders bread and cheese for them all, and pays for it herself.

Jane is confused by the inscription she reads about her school.

Another girl, Helen Burns, explains. Lowood is a refuge for poor, homeless girls. Jane is appalled. Why has she been sent here, and not to a proper school?

1. abominable: revolting.
2. inedible: not fit to eat.

HARD TIMES

Jane soon learns that conditions at Lowood are terrible. There is little food, and the rooms are freezing cold.

The girls are always cold, tired and hungry. Many fall ill. They faint from weakness during long prayer meetings.

On Sundays, they have to walk miles through the snow to church.

Miss Temple encourages them, but the other teachers are cruel. The girls are punished severely, and Helen Burns is beaten for things that are not her fault.

Later, Jane finds Helen sitting alone, reading. Jane is still angry at the teachers' cruelty and unfairness, but Helen is meek and patient.

Helen believes she must suffer in silence. Otherwise she may lose her chance to learn, correct her faults, and help others. Jane does not agree!

1. fare: food.

Love your enemies!

Would you not be happier if you tried to forget her severity?[1]

Helen tries to convince Jane that she should try to please even the nastiest teachers. They talk of Mrs. Reed, too. Helen wants Jane to forgive Mrs. Reed for her cruelty.

My mission is to mortify[2] these girls...to teach them to clothe themselves with shamefacedness and sobriety...

One day, Mr. Brocklehurst, the master who owns the school, makes a visit of inspection. He finds fault with everything! While he is droning on and on, Jane's slate[3] slips from her fingers...

CRASH! SMASH!

You must be on your guard against her...avoid her... punish her!

Mr. Brocklehurst turns on Jane in fury. He makes her stand, in disgrace, on a stool—and tells the whole school that she is a wicked liar!

1. her severity: Mrs. Reed's cruelty.
2. mortify: embarrass.
3. slate: thin sheet of shiny stone, used to write on.

A DEADLY SPRINGTIME

Jane is distraught, but Helen smiles at her secretly. This gives Jane courage. Afterwards, Jane cries bitterly, and Helen comforts her.

So does Miss Temple, who comes to find them as soon she can. She leads them both to her cozy private parlor.

There, Miss Temple listens while Jane tells the whole story of her short, unhappy life.

Then Miss Temple asks Helen very kindly about her health. With a worried look, she takes Helen's pulse.[1]

After this, it's time for tea and toast. As a special treat, Miss Temple produces a splendid cake, and cuts generous slices for the girls.

When tea is over, all three sit happily by the fire. Helen and Miss Temple talk of wonderful faraway countries, exciting books and poems, and the marvels of nature.

Listening to them inspires Jane to work hard at her studies. She wants to learn more!

Miss Temple gives Jane extra time for her favorite subjects: French and drawing. She begins to feel happier.

14   1. Takes Helen's pulse: counts how fast Helen's heart is beating by feeling the artery on her wrist. A fast or slow pulse can be a sign of illness.

At last, the weather gets warmer. Flowers grow quickly in the boggy land[1] around the school. So do dangerous germs! Half the girls fall ill…

… and many of them die! Mr. Brocklehurst—the coward!—stays away, but Miss Temple bravely nurses her pupils.

But even Miss Temple's loving care cannot save Helen. Her disease is deadly!

Very poorly!

Are you awake?

You came to say goodbye....

Jane knows that Helen is very, very ill. She desperately wants to see her. Helen's nurses try to send Jane away….

…. but she creeps into Miss Temple's room, where Helen is being looked after.

Helen looks terribly thin and pale, but she is calm and smiling. Helen believes that she is going to God, who loves her.

Goodnight… Goodnight…

Jane is heartbroken. She does not want to lose her good, kind friend. She climbs onto Helen's bed, and wraps her arms around her.

That is how Miss Temple finds them. Both are very peaceful. Jane is asleep but Helen has died.

1. boggy land: swamp land, often prone to breed disease in the springtime.

MOVING ON

After all the deaths, Lowood is rebuilt. It is warmer and cleaner, with plenty of good, healthy food. The teachers are kinder, and the pupils are happier.

I am the first[1] girl in the first class.

Helped by Miss Temple, Jane works hard at her studies. She is a clever girl, and, after six years, knows enough to become a teacher herself.

Two years later, Miss Temple make a surprise announcement. She's leaving to get married!

A new place...in a new house...among new people!

Jane wants to leave too. She feels trapped and restless. Lowood now seems like a prison. She wants to see more of the world!

Bravely, she puts an advertisement in the newspaper—and receives a reply!

A governess is wanted at a country house called Thornfield Hall. It's not far from Gateshead, so Jane calls in to see her old nursemaid, Bessie.

Bessie is now married, with a son—and a daughter who is called Jane! She has news of the Reed family:

Georgiana has tried to elope[2]—a disgrace—and John is often drunk—a disappointment!

Mrs. Reed is "not easy in her mind." In fact, she's despairing.

1. first: top.
2. elope: run away with a partner.

Alone in the world....

More shocking news follows...

Seven years ago, Jane's uncle, her father's brother, who lives abroad, called at Gateshead. He wanted to find Jane, but Mrs. Reed would not help him.

Jane travels on, to Thornfield Hall. She's excited, but very nervous. Aged just 18, and all alone—what future lies ahead?

At last, the journey ends.

Thornfield now!

I will do my best...let[1] the worst come to the worst, I can advertise again!

Will you walk this way, Ma'am?

A maid opens the door. Tired and anxious, but relieved that her journey is over, Jane enters her new home.

They pass through a wide, handsome hall.

Cozy...! Agreeable...!

How do you do, my dear?

The maid shows Jane into a private sitting room, where Mrs. Fairfax, the housekeeper, is waiting beside a warm and welcoming fire.

1. let: if.

A New Home

Mrs. Fairfax tells Jane about Thornfield Hall, then leads her upstairs to a pleasant, comfortable bedroom.

Jane meets her pupil—Adèle Varens. Adèle is the daughter of Mr. Rochester, owner of Thornfield. Adèle's mother, who came from Paris, is dead.

Adèle is pretty and charming but rather silly. She speaks mostly French. Jane must teach her better English, and help her to grow more sensible.

Adèle is easy to teach. Mrs. Fairfax is friendly and helpful. She shows Jane around the great house, and up onto the roof terrace to gaze at the view.

Jane hears mad laughter from upstairs.

Mrs. Fairfax blames the noises on Grace Poole. Grace is a woman who mends clothes in the attic. As they speak, Grace appears.

1. C'est ma gouvernante?: Is this my governess?

18   2. directions: instructions.

Restlessness is in my nature.

A Gytrash?[1] No—a traveler!

When her duties are done, Jane loves to escape from Thornfield and wander in the lanes nearby. One cold winter's evening, a huge dog bounds past her, followed by a man on horseback.

With a sickening crash, the horse skids on a patch of ice and falls!

Are you injured, sir?

Can I do anything? I am the governess!

Stand aside!

In spite of his protests, Jane helps the fallen rider to his feet. He limps over to his horse, and rides off into the darkness.

Thank you!

!!!!

Jane hurries home to look for Mrs. Fairfax. She is not in her room—but the traveler's huge dog is, looking quite at home in front of the fire.

1. Gytrash: fairytale monster, seen at dusk.

MR. ROCHESTER'S STORY

Yes! The traveler is none other than Mr. Rochester, owner of Thornfield Hall. He's visiting to discuss business with his farm manager, and to see Adèle.

Mr. Rochester invites Jane and Mrs. Fairfax to tea.

Let Miss Eyre be seated![1]

[A face] more remarkable for character than beauty...

Who are your parents? Have you seen much society?[2] Have you read much?

Jane observes Mr. Rochester carefully. He's a strange man: clever, moody, unpredictable, and sometimes rude.

He is very changeful and abrupt!

I am so accustomed to his manner that I never think of it.

Jane is surprised by Mr. Rochester's sharp way of speaking. Mrs. Fairfax explains that Mr. Rochester's temper has been soured by a terrible family quarrel.

Mr. Rochester never forgave his father, or spoke to him ever again.

He has great, dark eyes...very fine.

Jane is not like most other women. Mr. Rochester senses that she's straightforward, honest, and sincere. He can trust her! Jane is puzzled by him, but fascinated, also.

1. be seated: this shows unusual respect towards a governess like Jane.
2. seen much society: met many different people.

One day, Jane is taking Adèle for a walk. They meet Mr. Rochester. While Adèle plays with the dog, Mr. Rochester decides to tell Jane his life history.

They talk of all kinds of things—work and freedom, sin and forgiveness, pleasure, sorrow, goodness, and beauty. Jane speaks her mind freely, even though Mr. Rochester is her employer.

After the quarrel with his father, Mr. Rochester ran away to France. There he met a dancer, Céline Varens, and fell in love with her.

But Céline deceived him, took his money, and went off with another man.

Mr. Rochester challenged the other man to a duel, and wounded him. Céline ran away, leaving Adèle behind.

Now Céline is dead. Rochester does not know whether he is really Adèle's father, but feels he must look after her.

1. gregarious and communicative: sociable and talkative.

ARSON OR ACCIDENT?

Jane lies awake, thinking about Mr. Rochester. Then, what's that? A mad laugh! Footsteps! A strange smell!

Smoke! Flames! Jane leaps out of bed and rushes towards the smoke. The fire is in Mr. Rochester's room!

Jane quickly throws water from the washstand[2] onto the blaze. Mr. Rochester groans, and opens his eyes.

Jane tells Mr. Rochester about the laugh, the footsteps, and the fire. Mr. Rochester looks grim.

Mr. Rochester heads for the attic.

After a while, Mr. Rochester returns, pale and gloomy. He tells Jane not to talk about what has just happened.

Mr. Rochester sends Jane back to her room. But first, he clasps her by the hand and thanks her—passionately—for saving him.

1. doleful: miserable.
2. washstand: bedroom furniture; a stand for a washbasin and a big jug of water.

Back in her own bed, Jane soon falls fast asleep. Her dreams are strange and troubling—but very sweet.

Jane walks past Mr. Rochester's open door.

The servants clean up after the fire. Jane longs to see Mr. Rochester again—but is apprehensive about meeting him too.

Grace Poole is sitting calmly in Mr. Rochester's room, sewing new curtains!

Has anything happened here?

Jane decides she must question Grace Poole. Is Grace the would-be murderer?

He fell asleep with his candle lit!

Perhaps you may have heard a noise?

In reply, Grace invents a story—then asks some questions of her own.

I am certain I heard a laugh...

You must have been dreaming!

Grace is good at keeping secrets. She won't tell Jane what she knows.

Mr. Rochester has, on the whole, had a favorable day for his journey.

Mrs. Fairfax invites Jane to her room. They drink tea, and talk about the weather.

Journey! Has Mr. Rochester gone anywhere? I did not know he was out!

The ladies are very fond of him.

He is very likely to stay a week or more.

Mr. Rochester has gone to visit some fine, fashionable friends who live many miles away.

1. past comprehension: beyond understanding.

ALONE AT THE PARTY

How dare you! Poor stupid dupe![1]

Governess, disconnected,[2] poor and plain.

An accomplished[3] lady of rank.

Two weeks later...

Alone in her room, Jane feels terrible. How could she have let herself think that Mr. Rochester cared for her?

Painfully aware of her plain looks and her lowly position, Jane draws two portraits.

Mr. Rochester writes to tell Mrs. Fairfax that he is bringing his friends to Thornfield. All the servants, including Jane, work hard to get the house ready.

She understands what she has to do—nobody better.

Only Grace Poole seems not to care. She continues with her duties, as usual. Jane wonders what these are—the other servants seem to know.

Three days later Mr. Rochester and his friends arrive in fine style. Jane and Adèle—who is very excited—watch from behind a curtain.

Mr. Rochester evidently prefers her to any of the other ladies.

And she him!

That evening, there is a splendid party.

Beautiful Blanche Ingram is the belle of the ball. Next day, Jane and Mrs. Fairfax see her out riding with Mr. Rochester.

1. dupe: fool.
2. disconnected: with no friends or family.
24 3. accomplished: skillful at music, dancing, art, and elegant conversation.

What a love of a child!

Bonjour, mesdames.[1]

That night, Jane and Adèle are invited to join the guests. There are eight other women at the party. Mr. Rochester talks and laughs with them all.

Where is Mr. Rochester?

He makes me love him, without looking at me.

Adèle loves meeting new people, but Jane finds a quiet, hidden place just to sit and watch.

It's agony for Jane to see Mr. Rochester paying attention to the other young women.

He is not of their kind. I feel akin to him!

Jane listens to the young women chatter about the governesses who once taught them. Their words are thoughtless, cruel, and insulting.

Blanche Ingram plays the piano, while Mr. Rochester sings. He has a deep, splendid voice. Jane is thrilled.

What is the matter? Return!

I am tired, sir.

Jane can bear it no longer. She leaves the room—and Mr. Rochester follows.

Goodnight, my...

Jane begins to cry. Mr. Rochester starts to speak, but stops, suddenly. Jane retires to bed.

MR. ROCHESTER'S VISITOR

One night, they play charades.[1] Mr. Rochester chooses Blanche for his team, and she plays the part of a bride.

Miss Ingram is mine, of course!

Jane looks on, horrified.

He is going to marry her!

Blanche is proud and vain and Jane thinks she is mean, selfish, and spiteful. She does not truly love Mr. Rochester; she's just hoping to find a rich husband.

Jamaica...Kingston ... Became acquainted with Mr. Rochester...Old friend...

A visitor arrives—Mr. Mason has just landed in England from his home in the Caribbean.[2] Jane can't quite make out what he is saying.

I go first!

Jane tries to hear more. But Mr. Mason's words are interrupted. A mysterious old fortune-teller has arrived to offer her services. Blanche sees her first.

She returns, looking upset. The fortune-teller has hinted that Mr. Rochester will soon be poor!

She told us such things!

She knows all about us!

1. charades: a party game involving silent acting.
2. Caribbean: an island region east of the Gulf of Mexico.

26

The old woman insists that Jane goes to see her. Jane does not believe in fortune-telling, but is curious and excited.

The old woman says that Jane needs the warmth of love and friendship. She declares that Jane is lovesick—but afraid of revealing her love!

The old woman examines Jane's face carefully.

Suddenly, the old woman's voice changes. She takes off her hat….

Jane is not pleased. It's Mr. Rochester in disguise. Why? Was it a trick? A joke? A test?

As Mr. Rochester removes his disguise, Jane tells him that a visitor has arrived.

All at once, Mr. Rochester turns deathly pale. He gasps and staggers!

1. I have no faith: I do not trust you.
2. dare censure: face blame and shame.

27

A Mysterious Night

Grrrrrrrrrr! Haaaaaah-hah!

Good God! What a cry!

It's past midnight, but Jane is still awake. As she gazes out of the window, a blood-curdling shriek shatters the silence.

What is it?

A servant has had a nightmare; that is all.

All the guests are awoken and rush out. Mr. Rochester tells them not to worry, and sends them back to their rooms.

Come this way... Make no noise...

However, Jane gets dressed. As she half-expects, Mr. Rochester taps at her door.

You don't turn sick at the sight of blood?

Mr. Rochester unlocks a hidden door.

A man lies propped on pillows in the attic room. It is Mr. Mason —bleeding and unconscious!

What crime is this?

Mr. Rochester leaves Jane to look after Mr. Mason, but forbids her to speak to him.

But is he fit to move, sir?

At daybreak, the doctor arrives. Mr. Rochester orders him to bandage Mr. Mason's wounds and get him ready for a long journey.

I warned you!

The surgeon examines Mr. Mason, who is trembling and terrified. Mason has lost a lot of blood, but should survive.

She bit me! She sucked the blood! She's done for me, I fear!

Trembling, Mr. Mason sips medicine, and is soon able to stand.

The surgeon and Mr. Rochester help Mr. Mason totter towards his carriage. A few words escape his weak lips.

Jane does not understand. As the carriage rumbles away, Mr. Rochester leads her quietly into the garden.

They talk. Jane says that she was afraid of the shrieking and laughing. Was Grace Poole behind that door?

Mr. Rochester says that danger will come not from Grace Poole, but from Mr. Mason.

Again, Jane is puzzled. But she listens while Mr. Rochester tells her how he once made a terrible mistake, and is still suffering because of it.

Now, he wants peace and happiness—but getting this will cause a shameful scandal. Jane tells him, instead, to seek peace through God.

Suddenly, Rochester's voice changes. Now it is harsh and sarcastic.

He walks off to see his horses in the stables. Jane is left alone, shocked and shaken.

1. taints: pollutes.
2. regenerate: heal and reform.

GATESHEAD CALLS

Jane's dreams are strangely haunted by smiling little children. She remembers nursemaid Bessie saying that this was a sinister omen.

Mr. John—they say he killed himself!

A messenger appears with bad news: Jane's cousin John Reed has died. Mrs. Reed has collapsed from shock—and is calling for Jane.

You always said you had no relations!

Promise me only to stay a week!

Nine years ago, I left...I have yet[1] an aching heart.

Jane asks Mr. Rochester for permission to go. He has heard about the Reeds, and is surprised to learn that Jane is related to them. At last, Jane reaches Gateshead House.

How are you, dear aunt?

Mrs. Reed is very ill. She is confused, but she remembers Jane, and greets her very coldly.

Such a burden...so much annoyance.

Mrs. Reed talks bitterly about Jane's past life at Gateshead—and has some startling news for her!

"I wish to adopt her, and bequeath[2] her at my death whatever I may have."

Three years ago, a letter arrived from Jane's uncle, overseas. Mrs. Reed had hidden it, but now gives it to Jane—before she dies.

1. yet: still.
2. bequeath: give.

One day, Jane will be rich. But now she heads back to Thornfield Hall.

I am going back to Thornfield, but how long am I to stay there?

As Jane travels back, she wonders if Mr. Rochester has married Blanche Ingram. If he has, then she must leave Thornfield right away!

Hasten! Hasten! Be with him while you may!

She decides to walk the last few miles of the journey. The closer she gets to Thornfield, the happier she feels.

Go up home, and stay¹ your little weary wandering feet.

Wherever you are is my home!

Thoughts of Mr. Rochester fill Jane's mind. And then, by the side of the road—it's the man himself!

Time passes. Thornfield is quiet and calm. But why is there no news of Mr. Rochester's wedding? And no plan for the great occasion?

I have never loved him so well!

One beautiful midsummer evening, Mr. Rochester asks Jane to walk with him in the garden. Roses are blooming. Nightingales are singing.

I shall never see you again!

Mr. Rochester has important news. He is to marry Blanche Ingram in one month. Adèle must go to boarding school, and Jane must leave Thornfield!

1. stay: rest.

THE LOVERS UNITE

It is a long way off, sir. From *you*, sir.

I wish I had never been born!

You must stay!

Do you think I am a machine without feelings? Soulless and heartless? We stand at God's feet, equal—as we are!

Jane and Mr. Rochester sit under a shady tree. He offers to find her a new job as a governess, but the job is in Ireland.

Jane is almost too upset to speak. Mr. Rochester looks worried.

They kiss!

As we are!

So, Jane!

Let me go!

Jane, be still!

I am a free human being with an independent will.

Jane, come hither![1]

Jane, will you marry me? Will you be mine? Say yes, quickly!

Do you truly love me? Then, sir, I will marry you!

1. hither: here.

A wild wind springs up. Trees writhe and groan; lightning flashes overhead!

Adèle tells Jane that the big shady tree has been struck and shattered by lightning.

Jane hurries to greet Mr. Rochester. She has never, ever, felt so happy!

Mr. Rochester plans the wedding and the honeymoon. He wants to give Jane jewels, fine clothes….

But Mrs. Fairfax looks worried. Has Jane been foolish? Will Mr. Rochester change his mind?

All day, Jane works as a humble, dutiful governess. But, after work, she can be alone with Mr. Rochester, her future husband— and her equal.

1. are not accustomed: do not usually.

THE MYSTERY REVEALED

Two nights before the wedding, Jane has terrifying dreams of Thornfield Hall in ruins, and losing Mr. Rochester.

She wakes with a start. She sees light—a candle! Who's holding it? And what are they doing?

It's a strange woman with a wild face. She's trampling on Jane's wedding dress and ripping her veil. Jane faints with terror.

Torn from top to bottom!

Oh, to think what might have happened!

The wedding day

Look at yourself in the mirror!!

My brain is on fire with impatience!

In the morning, Jane tells Mr. Rochester about the damage. He shudders.

Adèle's French maid helps Jane put on her cleaned, mended wedding clothes.

Mr. Rochester cannot wait a moment longer. He hurries Jane to the church. She sees two strangers waiting outside, but does not stop to talk to them.

Wilt thou[1] take this woman for thy[2] wedded wife?

The marriage cannot go on!

!!!!!

Jane and Mr. Rochester stand ready to make their wedding vows. But the priest's mild voice is interrupted by angry words, spoken by one of the strangers.

1. Wilt thou: will you.
2. thy: your.

Jane's heart quakes. Mr. Rochester looks grim. The priest asks the stranger the reason for his interruption.

The stranger says that there is a witness to that wedding—who swears that Bertha is still alive.

The witness is Mr. Mason. He is Bertha's brother. He says Bertha attacked him when he visited Thornfield Hall.

Mr. Rochester confesses. Yes, he keeps Bertha hidden at Thornfield! He was tricked into marrying her by his father! Now she is cared for by Grace Poole.

They go to the attic.

Bertha hurls herself at Mr. Rochester, growling, biting, and scratching. She wants to kill him!

Dumbstruck and in a daze, Jane staggers to her room, alone—then falls to the floor, senseless.

RUNNING FROM LOVE

Jane wakes, sick and dizzy. Her mind is in turmoil. She staggers to her door, opens it —and falls into the arms of Mr. Rochester. He has been waiting for her, all night long!

Jane is too weak to stand. Mr. Rochester carries her downstairs, to sit beside the fire.

Mr. Rochester kneels beside Jane, and passionately tries to kiss her. Jane pushes him away.

Mr. Rochester says that his life with Bertha was a misery. Bertha was a demon; Jane is an angel! But Jane says that Bertha is ill, not evil. She needs help and understanding.

Mr. Rochester begs Jane to live with him in secret—and unmarried! Jane is afraid of his anger, but refuses. His plan is unjust, deceitful, dishonest!

1. Wound you thus: hurt your feelings in this way.
2. Caresses: kisses and affection.

That night, Jane dreams of her long-dead mother, who warns her to "flee temptation." She tiptoes away from Thornfield Hall before daybreak.

Jane takes a stagecoach to a distant town, where Mr. Rochester will not find her.

She begs for food and tries to find work, but fails.

Cold, tired, hungry, and fearful, Jane heads for the moors.[1] She spends the night under a bush; she begs for cold, stale porridge—pig food!

Jane wanders like a lost and starving dog.

Jane stumbles, exhausted across rough, boggy ground. Through the parsonage window, she sees two young women, reading.

Full of hope, Jane knocks at the parsonage door, but she is refused entry by an old servant.

Jane staggers away into the wild, rainy night.

1. moors: broad area of open land, often high but poorly drained, with patches of peat and heath.
2. parsonage: house for a priest.
3. All delicacy and cultivation: gentle, modest, ladylike, civilized.

Good News at Last

Later that night...

Jane has collapsed. A young man finds her and rescues her.

It is the priest! He takes Jane to the parsonage, where his sisters care for her tenderly.

The old servant—now kind and helpful—puts Jane to bed. She rests for a week, utterly exhausted.

The sisters, Diana and Mary, are sweet and friendly. But Jane cannot tell them her story. She's scared Mr. Rochester will find her.

Their brother, St. John, the priest, is clever, good —and handsome. Jane hides the truth from him, too…

…but offers to teach at the nearby church school. She wants to repay his kindness.

Sometimes, Jane wonders what her life would have been like if she had run away with Mr. Rochester. Her mind whirls ….

Jane wakes from her daydream. St. John arrives to ask how she likes the school. Then he tells her his great ambition. He wants to be a missionary!

Good evening!

A missionary, I resolve[1] to be!

A very pretty girl walks by. It is Rosamond Oliver, a rich heiress. She invites St. John to walk with her to her home. He blushes, but refuses.

Jane?

A letter arrives.

St. John's uncle, Mr. Eyre, has died—and left all his fortune to a niece, called Jane Eyre.

Oh! I am glad—I am glad!

St. John guesses who Jane is. She is his cousin—their mothers were sisters—and, thanks to their uncle, she's now an heiress!

Five thousand to each!

With Diana and Mary, St. John welcomes Jane into their family. She says she will share her fortune with them.

We must be married!

Now St. John has money to travel abroad as a missionary. He asks Jane to go with him…

What of Mr. Rochester? How and where is he?

Jane admires St. John but does not love him. She will be his helper, but she will not marry him.

Jane! Jane! Jane!

Then, in her head, she hears a voice calling! It's Mr. Rochester! Jane leaves for Thornfield, right away.

I am coming! Wait for me!

1. resolve: intend.

Endings and Beginnings

After 36 anxious hours Jane reaches Thornfield Hall. To her horror, she finds a blackened, crumbling ruin.

The silence of death.

A dreadful calamity!

Jane hurries to the nearest village. The innkeeper tells her what happened:

Bertha!

Last autumn, Bertha had set fire to Jane's old bedroom.

Grrrrrrrr! Eeeeeeeeeeeeeee!!!

Mr. Rochester tried to save her, but she jumped—to her death.

The fire blinded Mr. Rochester; falling beams crushed one of his arms.

I pity him!

Where is he?

Now Mr. Rochester lives alone and miserable, with his dog.

It is my master! Desperate and brooding— a caged eagle!

The innkeeper's boy drives Jane to a bleak, remote farmhouse. Jane waits outside, watching…

Jane plans a surprise.

Jane knocks on the door. Mary, an old servant, answers.

When Mr. Rochester calls for water, Jane brings it to him. The dog recognizes her at once.

Softly, Jane tells Mr. Rochester that Mary is in the kitchen.

Fearing that Jane's a ghost, Mr. Rochester reaches out to try to catch her.

Together again at last, they kiss passionately.

The years pass…

The wedding takes place three days later. A blissful future beckons; life seems like one long honeymoon.

St. John goes to India; his sisters marry. Adele learns to like lessons; Mrs. Fairfax retires. And Jane and Mr. Rochester? Eventually his sight returns. They have a baby son. And they are "ever together."

The End 41

CHARLOTTE BRONTË (1816–1855)

Charlotte Brontë belonged to an extraordinary literary family. Together with her two younger sisters, Anne and Emily, she created some of the best-loved and most famous novels ever written in English.

Charlotte's father, Patrick, was born in Ireland, but moved to work as a rector (senior priest) in the north of England. Although he loved books and learning, Patrick Brontë could not afford comfortable housing, good clothes, or a horse and carriage for his family. Instead, he expected all of his six children to work hard to make a living. He sent the girls to charity schools to learn reading, writing, and arithmetic. With these simple skills, Charlotte became a teacher in 1835, then, from 1839 to 1841, a governess. She worked in rich families' homes, where she was scorned for her lowly social status—just like Jane Eyre.

Charlotte Brontë: an engraving of a painting by Evert A. Duycknick, based on a drawing by George Richmond.

LOVE AND LEARNING

In 1842, Charlotte planned to open her own school. But no pupils came, and so she traveled to Brussels, Belgium, to improve her knowledge of French. She returned to Brussels in 1843 to work as a teacher of English. Charlotte fell in love with a Belgian headmaster there named Constantin Heger, but he was married and she did not tell him of her feelings. Instead, she wrote private, passionate letters to him—which the headmaster ripped up. His wife retrieved them from the wastepaper bin and meticulously glued them back together. They were later given to the British Museum by Heger's son.

EARLY WORKS

In 1845, Charlotte returned to England and read some of the poems that her sister Emily had been writing. She was so impressed that she arranged for them to be published in 1846, together with poems written by herself and her youngest sister, Anne. The sisters feared that their work would be scorned if readers knew they were women, so they chose false names: Acton (Anne), Ellis (Emily), and Currer (Charlotte) Bell. Their book sold only two copies, but was praised by influential people. This gave the sisters courage to go on writing. Charlotte also tried—but failed—to get her first novel, *The Professor*, published.

JANE EYRE

In 1846, Charlotte began work on her second novel, *Jane Eyre*. Although Jane Eyre's life story was very different from her own, Charlotte poured some of her deepest feelings into the text, and based several scenes on her own experiences. This—and her passionate, powerful writing—gave the story great appeal. It soon found a publisher, and became an overnight success. Charlotte and her sisters became celebrities. They traveled to London and Manchester to meet famous writers and thinkers.

Charlotte wrote two more novels: *Shirley* (1849), set against a background of industrial unrest in a Yorkshire village during the Napoleonic wars, and *Villette* (1852), about a sheltered girl who grows into a lonely young woman, until she finds her own place in the world.

STRONG VALUES

Charlotte had strong opinions about politics, society, and religion, and was not afraid to share them. She believed in traditional values, like honor, duty, respect, and hard work, and upheld law and order. She valued honesty, truthfulness, and straight-talking much more than the rules of rich, fashionable society. She was fiercely critical of religious hypocrites and fundamentalists.

Charlotte was physically very small. She was less than five feet tall, thin, shy, with plain features and poor eyesight. But she had a great spirit, a fine intellect, and an attractive personality. Her female friends were devoted to her, and she received several proposals of marriage from men.

FAMILY MATTERS

Charlotte enjoyed huge literary success, but her private life was tragic. Her mother died young, in 1821, when Charlotte was five years old. Her two older sisters, Elizabeth and Maria, died aged 10 and 12, just four years later. They were victims of tuberculosis (TB), a common 19th-century disease. Charlotte claimed that the hunger, cold, and dirt at their boarding school helped kill them, and stunted her own development.

In 1848 and 1849 Charlotte's two younger sisters, Anne and Emily, also died, very young, of tuberculosis. Her only brother, Branwell, was addicted to alcohol. He involved the family in several scandals, and died of both drink and disease, in 1848.

CHARLOTTE'S DEATH

In 1854, Charlotte married a poor curate (junior priest) named Arthur Bell Nicholls. At first her father forbade the marriage, but Charlotte and Arthur were very happy. Soon, Charlotte became pregnant, and fell seriously ill with continuous sickness and faintness. Some say the cause was pneumonia. Charlotte and her unborn child died in March 1855; she was only 38 years old.

However, following her death, evidence emerged which suggests that Charlotte actually died from typhus she may have caught from Tabitha Ackroyd, the Brontë household's oldest servant, who died shortly before her.

Charlotte is buried in the family vault, along with her father, brother, and sisters, in the church of St Michael and All Angels, Haworth, West Yorkshire.

BRITISH WOMEN'S EDUCATION AND LEGAL RIGHTS

Charlotte Brontë lived a very respectable, conventional life, and spent years as a teacher and governess. Her writings, however, reveal her passionate belief in personal freedom and equality, and convey her complaints about the low standard of women's education.

The character Jane Eyre describes herself as "free-born" and "independent." Jane becomes a governess because teaching is the only career, apart from marriage, open to "decent" women. Throughout the book, Jane respects herself and has the courage to stand up for her beliefs and ideas at a time when women had very few legal rights or educational opportunities.

EDUCATION AND MARRIAGE

During the 1800s, most British children did not go to school. Rich parents paid to send boys and girls to private schools, or employed governesses; churches and charities ran schools for a few poor children. In many schools, standards were low and children were badly treated. Girls were not usually taught the same subjects as boys, but were expected to learn useful skills, such as sewing, that they might need as wives and mothers.

Unmarried women were under the legal control of their fathers. The law allowed married women's husbands to beat them, lock them up, and take their children away from them. Husbands had the right to control their wives' money and property—even their clothes.

Divorce was almost impossible. Marriages could only be ended by a private Act of Parliament (a special new law). The new Poor Law banned and punished beggars and wanderers seeking shelter and employment.

1792
Female writer Mary Wollstonecraft publishes *A Vindication of the Rights of Women*, calling for equal rights with men. Her ideas are shocking, and ignored by most men—and many women.

1836–1858
Working-class campaigners, called "Chartists," demand social justice. There are riots in the north of England. Poor, homeless people—like Jane Eyre when she runs away—are treated with suspicion.

1839
Thanks to campaigns by female writer Caroline Norton (1818–1877), women win the right of custody (care and control) over their children under seven years old, and rights to see their older children, even if their husbands have taken them away.

1840
Women governesses outnumber male school teachers.

1848
Queens College, London, is set up to train women teachers.

1854
Cheltenham Ladies' College (private boarding school) is set up in south-west England. It aims to teach women the same subjects that boys learn at the best boys' schools, to the same high standards. Soon, other private schools for girls follow its example.

1857
Divorces are now handled by legal courts. Wives can ask for a divorce from husbands who are cruel, who desert them, or who have affairs with other women.

1860
Florence Nightingale sets up Nightingale School to train women as expert, professional nurses.

1867
The London Society for Women's Suffrage is formed to campaign for the right to vote for women.

1870
The Education Act is established. Local councils must provide elementary (primary) schools for all children, rich or poor.

1870 and **1884**
New laws give wives the right to keep the clothes, money, and other property they owned before marriage, and to run their own businesses.

1874
Elizabeth Garrett Anderson and Sophia Jex-Blake set up the London School of Medicine for Women.

1876
A new law allows women in Britain to train as doctors.

1878
Wives who leave cruel husbands win the right to demand financial support for their children. British universities accept female students for the first time.

1879
Millicent Fawcett founds the National Union of Women's Suffrage Societies to organize a country-wide campaign for votes for women.

1880
Primary education is made mandatory for all British children. Children from rich families go to private schools; poor, ordinary children go to state schools.

1886
A new law gives a widow complete custody of her children after her husband dies.

1891
Married women can no longer be forced by the law to stay in their husband's house against their will.

1895
Judges can now order protection for women who have been attacked by violent husbands.

1899
Both boys and girls must by law attend school until age 12.

BRONTË FAMILY TIMELINE

April, 1814
Maria, the first of the Brontë siblings, is born.

February, 1815
Elizabeth Brontë is born.

April, 1816
Charlotte Brontë is born.

June, 1817
Branwell, the only boy in the Brontë family, is born.

July, 1818
Emily Brontë is born.

January, 1820
The last of the Brontës, Anne, is born.

1821
Maria Brontë, Charlotte's mother, dies of cancer.

1843
Charlotte travels to Brussels to teach English.

1846
Poems by Currer, Ellis, and Acton Bell is published, but sells only two copies.

1847
Jane Eyre is published and becomes an instant hit. Emily Brontë's *Wuthering Heights* is published.

1848
Anne Brontë's *The Tenant of Wildfell Hall* is published.
(December) Emily dies of tuberculosis.

1849
Anne dies.
Branwell dies of suspected consumption.
Charlotte's novel *Shirley* published.

1853
Charlotte's novel *Villette* is published.

1854
Charlotte marries curate Arthur Bell Nicholls.

1855
Charlotte suffers from poor health while pregnant, and dies along with her unborn child.

1857
Two years after Charlotte's death, her first novel, *The Professor,* is published.

BRONTË'S BOOKS

t seems as if Charlotte was born to be a writer. While still a child, she and her brother and sisters made up stories and wrote over 20 books about imaginary lands called Glass Town and Angria. Charlotte also kept a diary, and wrote long, lively letters to her friends. Aged 20, she bravely wrote to the Poet Laureate (official national poet) asking for advice on how to earn her living as a writer. Discouragingly, he wrote back, saying, "Literature cannot be the basis of a woman's life, and it ought not to be." This did not, however, keep Charlotte from writing!

Charlotte Brontë's books:
1846: *Poems by Currer, Ellis and Acton Bell*
1846: *The Professor* (at first unpublished)
1847: *Jane Eyre*
1849: *Shirley*
1852: *Villette*

Part of the original manuscript of Jane Eyre

WHAT THE CRITICS SAID

Jane Eyre was Charlotte Bronte's second novel. It won great praise and stirred up tremendous controversy. Most reviewers praised it, but a few were savage.

"a very clever book … varied and vivid"

"the most extraordinary production … true and interesting"

"freshness and originality"

"a mere vulgar boiling-over"

"the story invites the reader into the recesses of the human heart"

"do not leave it around for your daughters to read"

"much power, and still more promise…"

"a naughty book"

"we have rarely met with a more deeply interesting story"

"a new genius!"

ADAPTATIONS OF JANE EYRE

Over the decades, *Jane Eyre* has been adapted many times for films and plays all over the world. Some are period dramas that stick closely to Brontë's original tale; others are musicals, operas, and even horror films.

1910: *Jane Eyre* (USA)
This very early film was in black-and-white and had no script or soundtrack.

1914: *Jane Eyre* (USA)
Another black-and-white silent movie, directed by Frank Hall Crane, who played Mr. Rochester in the 1910 version.

Jane wanders the moors in Franco Zeffirelli's Jane Eyre, *1996*

1926: *Orphan of Lockwood* (Germany)
A German adaptation of *Jane Eyre*.

1940: *Rebecca* (USA)
Directed by Alfred Hitchcock, this film was based on a book of the same name, which was itself inspired by *Jane Eyre*. Jane was played by Joan Fontaine, who also starred in another more straightforward adaptation, made in 1944.

1943: *I Walked with a Zombie* (USA)
A horror film, inspired by *Jane Eyre* and loosely based on parts of Brontë's story.

1944: *Jane Eyre* (USA)
Director Robert Stevenson cast actor/director Orson Wells as Mr. Rochester and Joan Fontaine as Jane.

1956: *Mei gu* (Hong Kong)
(*The Orphan Girl*) A Japanese retelling of *Jane Eyre*, starring Lin Dai as Jane, who is known in this version as "Mei Ji."

1970: *Jane Eyre* (UK)
Starring Susanne York as Jane and George C. Scott as Mr. Rochester.

1994: *Jane Eyre* (UK)
Ballet adaptation, created by the London Children's Ballet.

1996: *Jane Eyre*
Directed by Franco Zeffirelli. Charlotte Gainsburg played Jane alongside supermodel Elle MacPherson, who played Jane's love rival Blanche Ingram.

2000: *Jane Eyre* (UK)
An opera, composed by Michael Berkeley.

There have also been numerous television adaptations. In the UK alone, the BBC has made seven drama series based on *Jane Eyre*; the earliest was televised in 1963, and the latest was aired in 2006.

INDEX

IF YOU ENJOYED THIS BOOK, YOU MIGHT LIKE TO TRY
THESE OTHER TITLES IN THE BARRON'S *GRAPHIC CLASSICS* SERIES:

Adventures of Huckleberry Finn

Dr. Jekyll and Mr. Hyde

Dracula

Frankenstein

Hamlet

The Hunchback of Notre Dame

Journey to the Center of the Earth

Julius Caesar

Kidnapped

Macbeth

The Man in the Iron Mask

Moby Dick

Oliver Twist

A Tale of Two Cities

The Three Musketeers

Treasure Island

Wuthering Heights